Thanksgiving Mice!

Thanksgiving Mice!

by **Bethany Roberts**

illustrated by **Doug Cushman**

Clarion Books • New York

Clarion Books
a Houghton Mifflin Company imprint
215 Park Avenue South, New York, NY 10003
Text copyright © 2001 by Barbara Beverage
Illustrations copyright © 2001 by Doug Cushman

The illustrations were executed in watercolor.
The type was set in 16-point Palatino.

For information about permission to reproduce selections from this book,
write to Permissions, Houghton Mifflin Company,
215 Park Avenue South, New York, NY 10003.

www.houghtonmifflinbooks.com

Printed in the USA.

Library of Congress Cataloging-in-Publication Data

Roberts, Bethany.
Thanksgiving mice! / by Bethany Roberts ; illustrated by Doug Cushman.
p. cm.
Summary: A group of mice have some problems when they put on a play to commemorate
the first Thanksgiving, but everything works out all right in the end.
ISBN 0-618-12040-8
[1. Mice—Fiction. 2. Thanksgiving Day—Fiction. 3. Theater—Fiction. 4. Stories in rhyme.]
I. Cushman, Doug, ill. II. Title.
PZ8.3.R5295 Th 2001
[E]—21   00-047456

WOZ 10 9 8 7 6 5 4 3

To Jennifer, with thanksgiving!
—B.R.

To all my family and friends, for whom I'm thankful every day.
—D.C.

Thanksgiving mice
get ready for a show.

Costumes! Sets!
Go, go, go!

Practice lines!
Curtains! Props!

Hurry, hurry!
Oh, no, no!

Thanksgiving mice
shout, "Have a seat!"

"Come one, come all!
Come see our play!"

11

Pilgrim mice sailed on a ship.

They came from England, far away.

"Raise the anchor!"
"Set the sails!"

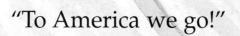
"To America we go!"

For many days the Pilgrim mice
in stormy seas tossed to and fro.

They huddled, seasick, in the hold,
hungry, thirsty, filled with dread.

At last their journey
came to an end.

The mice all shouted,
"Land ahead!"

They built new homes in tree trunks,
but felt too weak to sing.

For they were hungry, thin, and cold,

so they waited for the spring.

One day they met some friendly folks,
who gave them corn to sow.

They planted it and tended it,

and watched it grow and grow!

"Thanks to God!"
the mice all squeaked.

"We've lots to eat!
Hooray!"

And so they said
to their new friends,

"Let's feast! Let's dance!
Let's play!"

Thanksgiving mice all take a bow.

Clap! Clap! Clap!
Hurrah! Hooray!

31

"Come one, come all,
come feast with us—
on *this* Thanksgiving Day!"

The mice all shouted,
"Land ahead!"

They built new homes in tree trunks,
but felt too weak to sing.

For they were hungry, thin, and cold,

so they waited for the spring.

One day they met some friendly folks,
who gave them corn to sow.

They planted it and tended it,

and watched it grow and grow!

"Thanks to God!"
the mice all squeaked.

"We've lots to eat!
Hooray!"

And so they said
to their new friends,

"Let's feast! Let's dance!
Let's play!"

Thanksgiving mice all take a bow.

Clap! Clap! Clap!
Hurrah! Hooray!

31

"Come one, come all,
come feast with us—
on *this* Thanksgiving Day!"